Stars
for
Sarah

Stars for Sarah

BY ANN TURNER

PICTURES BY MARY TEICHMAN

📚 A Charlotte Zolotow Book

An Imprint of HarperCollins*Publishers*

The illustrations were prepared as acid etchings
on four copper plates using a color separation process.

Stars for Sarah
Text copyright © 1991 by Ann Turner
Illustrations copyright © 1991 by Mary Teichman
Printed in the U.S.A. All rights reserved.
Typography by Al Cetta
1   2   3   4   5   6   7   8   9   10
First Edition

Library of Congress Cataloging-in-Publication Data
Turner, Ann Warren.
    Stars for Sarah / by Ann Turner ; pictures by Mary Teichman.
        p.   cm.
    "A Charlotte Zolotow book."
    Summary: Lying in bed at night, Sarah wonders what life will be
like when she moves to her new house, and her mother comes and
reassures her.
    ISBN 0-06-026186-2 — ISBN 0-06-026187-0 (lib. bdg.)
    [1. Moving, Household—Fiction.   2. Mothers and daughters—
Fiction.]   I. Teichman, Mary, ill.   II. Title.
PZ7.T8535St   1991   89-26908
[E]—dc20   CIP
                                                                AC

For Charlotte, with love

—A.T.

For Marisa, Catherine, Liana,
Lizzie, and Matthew

—M.T.

Sarah woke one night.
The moon was full,
white and shining through the pine tree
outside her window.

The wind blew,
making tree shadows wave
on the wallpaper,
and Sarah sat up in bed.

She watched the moonlight on her spread,
her dolls all lined in a row,
and touched her roller skates under the bed.
And though the stars painted on the ceiling
shone down as always,

Sarah was scared.

"Mother!" Sarah called.

Mother came in
and sat on Sarah's bed.
"Will the new house be home?
Will all the things I like here
be there?"

Mother held her hand.
"Tell me all the things you like,
and I'll tell you which things
will be at the new house."

When you put me to bed,
and almost close the door, but not quite,
the light makes a path
out to where you are.
I can run on it when I am scared."
Mother said, "The light
will make a path through the doorway,
and we will be there when you are scared."

"When the wind blows and the moon shines,
the tree makes waves on the wallpaper,
and there is a cricket that sings
on my windowsill."
Mother patted her hand.
"There is an oak tree by your window
at the new house,
and when the wind blows and the moon shines
you will have waves on the wallpaper
and moonlight on your bed.
But I can't promise a cricket will sing
on your windowsill."

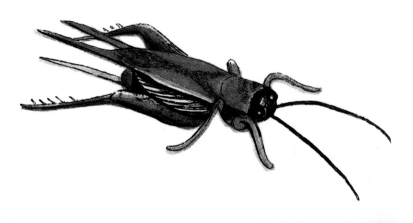

Sarah pointed to the bureau.

"Annabell, Josephine, Amanda, and Joey
have to sit together just like that.
That is the way my dolls sleep."

Mother smiled.

"We will put Annabell first, then Josephine,
and Amanda and Joey side by side,
and they will sleep leaning together."

Sarah reached under her bed.
"My roller skates live here,
waiting for me to play.
Will there be a hill to skate down
with the wind in my face?"
Mother said, "I can't promise there's a hill
to skate down with the wind in your face,
but your roller skates will be
under your bed, ready for play."

"What about Freddy?" Sarah said loudly.
"He taught me to make grass flutes
and fat bubble-gum bubbles

and spit in rain puddles.''

Mother sighed.

''There will never be another Freddy,

but a girl lives near the new house
who has a pet rabbit with a black nose."
"I could show her how to make grass flutes
and spit in rain puddles,"
Sarah said,
"but I will still miss Freddy."

Sarah lay back and looked at the ceiling.
"Will I have stars over my bed
at the new house?
When you kiss me goodnight and leave,
they glow and shine
and push the dark away."
Mother put her arms around Sarah.

"When we get to the new house,
we will find the girl
and meet the rabbit with the black nose.
We will put your skates under your bed,
line your dolls all in a row,
and wait for the moon to rise.
When the wind blows
you will have waves on your wallpaper
and moonlight on your bed."

"And stars on the ceiling?"

"We will paint stars for Sarah
on the ceiling,

and they will glow and shine
and push the dark away.''